Books should be returned on or before the
last date stamped below.

ABERDEENSHIRE
LIBRARIES

WITHDRAWN
FROM LIBRARY

ABERDEENSHIRE LIBRARY
AND INFORMATION SERVICE
MELDRUM MEG WAY, OLDMELDRUM

Bradman, Tony

Dilly and his swamp
lizard

JS

1046015

Other DILLY titles available

Dilly the Angel
Dilly and the Big Kids
Dilly Dinosaur, Detective
Dilly the Dinosaur
Dilly and the Ghost
Dilly Goes on Holiday
Dilly's Muddy Day
Dilly and the Pirates
Dilly Goes to School
Dilly Dinosaur, Superstar
Dilly and the Tiger
Dilly Tells the Truth
Dilly Goes Swamp Wallowing
Dilly and the Vampire

TONY BRADMAN

AND HIS SWAMP LIZARD

Illustrated by Susan Hellard

MAMMOTH

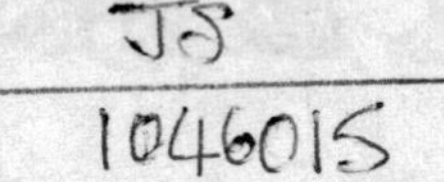
JS
1046015

First published in Great Britain 1991
by Piccadilly Press Ltd
Published 1993 by Mammoth
an imprint of Reed International Books Ltd
Michelin House, 81 Fulham Road, London SW3 6RB
and Auckland, Melbourne, Singapore and Toronto

Reprinted 1993 (twice), 1994, 1995, 1996 (twice)

Text copyright © Tony Bradman 1991
Illustrations copyright © Susan Hellard, 1991

The right of Tony Bradman to be identified as Author
and of Susan Hellard to be identified as illustrator of this work
has been asserted by them in accordance with the Copyright,
Designs and Patents Act 1988.

ISBN 0 7497 0734 8

A CIP catalogue record for this title
is available from the British Library

Printed and bound in Great Britain
by Cox & Wyman Ltd, Reading, Berkshire

This paperback is sold subject to the condition
that it shall not, by way of trade or otherwise,
be lent, resold, hired out, or otherwise circulated
without the publisher's prior consent in any form
of binding or cover other than that in which
it is published and without a similar condition
including this condition being imposed
on the subsequent purchaser.

Contents

Dilly Goes to the Museum

"Can I get down from the table now, Father?" said Dilly. "It's almost time for *Swamp Mania*!"

Dilly and I usually watch TV on Saturday after breakfast. *Swamp Mania* is on every week, and it's terrific. It's like lots of different programmes all rolled into one.

There are serials, quizzes, music and interviews with pop stars. A presenter called Donna also does things about

science, and how we can stop pollution. I like those.

Dilly, of course, only likes the cartoons, especially the noisy ones with plenty of fighting.

"Actually, Dilly," said Father, "you can go and brush your teeth and get dressed. You won't be watching any television today. Don't you remember? We're going to the museum to help Dorla with her project."

I'm very interested in endangered species. So this term I decided to do my school project on Marsh Moths. Mother found out there was a special exhibition at the museum about them.

I've really been looking forward to seeing it.

"I think Marsh Moths are stupid, and I don't *want* to go to the smelly museum," said Dilly. "I'll miss *Dinosaur Warriors*, and it's my *favourite*."

"Well, it will do you good to miss it for once," said Father. "You spend far too much time in front of that TV as it is."

Dilly argued for a while longer. But in the end, he had to do what Father said. He stomped upstairs, STOMP, STOMP, STOMP. He went into the bathroom and shut the door with a . . . SLAM!

When we arrived at the museum, we got our tickets, then left our coats in the cloakroom. Everywhere was crowded, and there was a big queue for the Marsh Moths exhibition. So

Mother said we should go there last.

We stood in front of the big map in the entrance hall.

"Umm, I don't know where to start . . ." said Father. He put his paw on Dilly's shoulder and smiled at him. "What do *you* want to see, Dilly?" he said.

"*Dinosaur Warriors*," he muttered. Father's smile disappeared.

"Don't you *ever* give up, Dilly?" he sighed. "I've already told you, you're *not* going to see *Dinosaur Warriors* today, so just forget about it. Now try to enjoy yourself, will you?"

But Dilly had decided he didn't want to. He sulked, and he sulked, and he sulked.

And that wasn't all he did. He dragged his feet, so Mother and Father had to keep telling him to come along. His shoelaces seemed to come undone every five minutes, too.

He kept saying he wanted a drink, so in the end we went to the museum cafe. Dilly made a disgusting noise with his pineapple juice, then he spilt it down his front. Everyone stared.

"Oh, Dilly," said Mother, dabbing at his dungarees. "Now look what you've done!"

"I don't care," said Dilly with a scowl.

I could tell Mother and Father were getting cross. I was pretty fed up with Dilly myself. But then I knew what he was up to. He was trying as hard as he could to spoil our day just because he couldn't do what *he* wanted.

And so far he was succeeding.

We left the cafe and headed for the Human Hall. I think it's one of the best places in the museum. The human skeletons are fascinating. We all thought the models of those funny little human houses were very interesting, too.

All of us, that is, except Dilly.

"Dilly!" said Father. "What *do* you think you're doing?"

Mother and I looked round. Dilly was sitting in the middle of the floor.

"My legs are tired," he said in his sulkiest voice. "I don't want to walk

any more."

"Well, I'm afraid you'll have to," said Father. "We're going to see the Marsh Moths exhibition now. Come on, up you get."

Dilly didn't say anything. He just sat there with his I'm-Not-Going-To-Do-Anything-You-Tell-Me-To look on his face.

"I'm waiting, Dilly," said Father, who was losing his temper at last. He had his arms folded, and he was tapping his foot as he spoke.

But Dilly still didn't say anything. And he didn't stand up.

"Right," said Father. "I've had just about all I can take from you today, Dilly. You've done nothing but sulk since we got here. If you're not on your feet by the time I count to three, you'll be banned from ever watching *Dinosaur Warriors* again! One . . . two . . ."

I knew Father would never make it to three.

Dilly opened his mouth and . . . that's right, you guessed it, he let rip with an ultra-special, 150-mile-per-hour super-scream, the kind that makes everyone dive for cover, and human skeletons collapse into heaps of old bones.

And then he did something really unexpected. Before we could stop him, he got up, and scampered out of the door as fast as his little legs could carry him. They certainly didn't seem tired any more. The last thing we saw was his tail disappearing into the crowds.

"That little rascal," said Father through gritted teeth. He was angry, but now he looked worried, too. "I'll tan his hide when I find him . . ."

Finding Dilly, however, proved more difficult than we thought.

He wasn't at the special place where the museum attendants took lost dinosaurs. And none of the attendants had seen him, either.

In the end we decided to split up and search. Mother said we should all meet at the queue for the Marsh Moths exhibition in fifteen minutes.

I looked everywhere. I ran through the crowds calling Dilly's name. I was even beginning to get worried myself. Dilly can be a real pain, but he's still my brother.

There was no sign of him. I didn't have any more time, so I started making my way to the Marsh Moths exhibition. I just hoped Mother or Father had found him . . .

"Well, really!" I heard someone saying when I got there. "Did you see that small dinosaur? He just walked straight to the head of the queue and went in. It shouldn't be allowed!"

Somehow I knew who that small dinosaur was. I ran to the head of the queue, and dodged past the museum attendant at the door. Somebody called out, but I took no notice.

I was right, too. There was Dilly in front of me. But he wasn't alone. He was with several grown-up dinosaurs. A couple were holding big, bright lights, one was carrying a TV camera, and the one Dilly was talking to had a microphone.

And they were all wearing jackets

with the words *Swamp Mania* on them!

"So tell me, Dilly," the one with the microphone was saying. I recognised her straight away. It was Donna, my favourite presenter. "Are you interested in Marsh Moths?"

"Oh, yes," said Dilly. Liar, I thought. But then he gave me a surprise. "My big sister Dorla knows much more about them than me, though," he said. "That's her over there by the door."

I could feel myself going hot and green with embarrassment as Donna came towards me . . .

But everything was OK in the end. *Swamp Mania* had come to do an item about the exhibition, and I told them everything I knew about Marsh Moths. They said I was very helpful.

In fact, they were so impressed, they

asked me to go on the programme again when they do something else about conservation! I was so pleased I could hardly speak.

Mother and Father had arrived just after me, and they were very proud. Dilly was happy too. Donna gave him a special present – a *Dinosaur Warriors* T-shirt!

It didn't save him from a telling off on the way home, though. Mother and Father were still cross because he'd run off. They said it was a very dangerous thing to do.

"I'm sorry, Father," said Dilly. "I promise I'll never do it again."

But I wouldn't mind if he did . . . especially if he led us to something as interesting next time!

Dilly and the Girlfriend

"Oh, Dilly," said Mother. "You *are* naughty. What have you been up to?"

Dilly had just come in from the garden, and was standing on the mat inside the back door. He was looking down at his dungarees and shoes. They were covered in mud.

"I was only playing, Mother," he said. "I didn't *mean* to get dirty."

I knew that was a fib, although I didn't say anything. Dilly just *loves* getting in a mess. But Mother wasn't fooled, either. She was cross and told Dilly off. Dilly said he was sorry.

"I wouldn't mind so much, but that's the second lot of clothes you've had on today," she said. "I must spend half my life putting your things in the washing machine."

Just then the doorbell rang.

"You stay *right* where you are while I see who that is, Dilly," said Mother. "I don't want you walking mud all over the house."

She went to the front door and opened it. Two dinosaurs were standing there, one of whom we knew very well.

"Why, hello, Dan!" said Mother. "What a lovely surprise! And you've brought a friend . . . Come in, come in!"

Dan is Father's younger brother, and he's our favourite uncle. Dilly thinks he's wonderful, mostly because he doesn't mind playing the sort of rough games Dilly enjoys.

Uncle Dan introduced us to his friend. Her name was Darlene, and I thought she was really nice. She was very pretty, too.

Suddenly the kitchen door flew open, and Dilly came dashing out. He must have heard Uncle Dan's voice. I could see Mother wasn't pleased. Dilly had left a trail of muddy paw prints behind him.

"Uncle Dan! Uncle Dan!" he shouted. He ran over and tried to climb up Uncle Dan's leg. "Come on, let's play *fighting*!"

"Hold on a second, Dilly," said Uncle Dan. "There's someone I'd like you to meet. This is Darlene."

Dilly hadn't noticed Darlene yet. He stopped punching Uncle Dan and looked at her.

"Hello, Dilly," said Darlene. She gave him a big smile. "I've heard so much about you."

"It's all true," I said. Mother gave me a look, so I shut up.

Dilly didn't say a word. He just turned round and started punching Uncle Dan again.

"Stop that this instant, Dilly!" said Mother. She pulled him away. "Now where are your manners? Say hello to Darlene, and stop behaving like a little hooligan."

Dilly looked confused.

"But this is what I *always* do with Uncle Dan," he said.

"Well, you're not doing it today," said Mother. "I'm sure Darlene isn't interested in all that rough stuff. Now take off those muddy shoes, then go and change."

"Yes, Mother," said Dilly. He didn't sound very happy.

By the time Dilly came downstairs again, we were all having a drink. Mother had got out the best bone china cups, and the special fern cookies she saves for visitors. We talked for ages, and I thought it was a lot of fun.

But Dilly didn't.

He kept asking Uncle Dan to play with him. When Uncle Dan said he couldn't, Dilly sulked. And when it was time for Uncle Dan and Darlene to go, Dilly wouldn't say goodbye.

Mother said he had to, so he did exactly what you'd expect. He opened his mouth and . . . that's right, you guessed it, he let rip with an ultra-special, 150-mile-per-hour super-scream, the kind that makes visitors leave *very* quickly.

I knew Mother was going to give him a real telling off. She did, but she didn't send him to his room. And she made him promise never to be rude like that again.

"I know you like playing with Uncle Dan, Dilly," she said. "He likes playing with you, too. But he couldn't today because he was with Darlene."

"I hope he doesn't bring her next time he comes," said Dilly. He was still looking a little sulky.

"I bet he does," I said. "She's his *girlfriend*, silly Dilly."

"That will do, Dorla," said Mother, giving me her Don't-Upset-Dilly-Any-More look.

But I was right. Every time we saw Uncle Dan after that, he was with Darlene.

It was easy to see they liked each other a lot. They were always holding paws and looking into each other's eyes. I thought it was sweet. Dilly didn't like it a bit, though.

One day we saw them kissing. They were standing at the end of the garden, and didn't think anyone could see them. But Dilly and I were watching them through the window.

"Yuk!" said Dilly. He made his I-Think-I'm-Going-To-Be-Sick face. "I'll never do *that* when I'm grown-up."

"No one will want to kiss *you*, anyway," I said. Dilly just stuck his tongue out.

I knew what was wrong with him. He didn't like Darlene. He even said so one night at dinner. As far as he was concerned, all she did was stop Uncle Dan playing rough games.

The next week Uncle Dan and Darlene said they wanted to take both Dilly and me out. You can imagine how I felt.

"How about a visit to the park?" said Uncle Dan. "You'd like that, wouldn't you, Dilly?"

But Dilly didn't want to go. For a second I thought I wouldn't have to put up with him. It would be wonderful.

Mother, however, insisted. She said Dilly needed some fresh air. She also told me to keep an eye on him.

Thanks a lot, Mother, I thought.

We set off for the park. Dilly walked along with a scowl on his face and his paws behind his back. He wouldn't talk to Darlene, although she tried hard to be friendly.

"Oh, no!" said Uncle Dan just as we got to the park. "I think it's going to rain."

We looked up, and sure enough, there was a huge black cloud right above us. The first few fat drops were already slapping on the pavement. Soon the rain was pounding down.

"Come on, we'll have to run for it!" said Uncle Dan.

There were two shelters inside the park. Uncle Dan and I ran into one. Darlene and Dilly must have run into the other. We couldn't see them from where we were.

"I hope they're OK," said Uncle Dan.

He seemed a little worried. Suddenly I realised what he was thinking, and I started to worry too. What if Dilly was being horrible to Darlene?

The rain started to ease off at last. But then we heard a strange noise. It sounded like lots of splashing, and somebody laughing. I looked at Uncle Dan. Uncle Dan looked at me.

It didn't take us long to find the other two. We stood staring at them with our mouths open. Dilly and Darlene were stamping in all the puddles, and laughing their heads off!

"There you are!" said Darlene. "Isn't this fun?"

They were both drenched, and their shoes were covered in mud. So were

Dilly's dungarees and Darlene's jeans.

"I should have known," said Uncle Dan. He was laughing now too. "Darlene's always loved splashing in puddles and getting messy. She's as bad as you, Dilly."

"I know," said Dilly. "She ran out and started splashing as soon as she saw a puddle. She's *terrific*."

He gave Darlene a big smile, and she smiled back. That's when I noticed he was holding her paw . . .

Darlene turned out to be very

adventurous. She liked climbing trees and playing hide and seek in the rocks as much as she liked splashing. We had a really good time.

Mother didn't even tell us off for being messy. She just laughed when she heard what we'd been doing, and made us all a hot drink. Dilly sat on the sofa between Darlene and Uncle Dan as he drank his.

Later, at bedtime, I heard Dilly talking to Mother.

"Do you think Uncle Dan will *marry* Darlene?" he said.

"I don't know, Dilly," said Mother. "He might, I suppose."

"Well, if he doesn't," said Dilly, "*I* will."

Somehow I hoped that would never happen – for Darlene's sake!

DILLY AND HIS SWAMP LIZARD

"I *don't* belive it," said Mother. "Dilly, you've forgotten your lunch box *again*!"

It was home time, and we'd been waiting by the school gate for ages. Dilly was the last to come out, as usual.

"I'm sorry, Mother," said Dilly. He gave her his Please-Don't-Tell-Me-Off-I-Didn't-Really-Mean-It look.

"You're *so* forgetful at the moment," said Mother. "That's the third time you've left your lunch box at school this week." Then she smiled. "Maybe I'll tie a knot in your tail tomorrow so you'll remember. Now run back and get it. And don't be long . . . I've got a lot to do today."

Dilly did what he was told, and we were soon on our way home. We hadn't gone far when we saw a poster on a giant fern tree.

"What does it say, Dorla?" asked Dilly. I read it out.

SUNDAY FUN DAY
AT DINOSAUR PARK!
Come one, come all, and have a ball!
Rides, stalls, events –
Families welcome!
Pet Show starts 12 noon!

It sounded terrific, so I wasn't

surprised that Dilly got excited. But you should have seen him when I read out the list of events. I thought he was going to *explode*.

"Oh, wow!" he shouted. "Can we go, Mother? I want to put Swampy in for the pet show. I *know* he could win a prize!"

Swampy is Dilly's pet swamp lizard. Dilly thinks he's absolutely wonderful. I don't. But I didn't say anything.

"We'll see, Dilly," said Mother. "I'll talk it over with your Father this evening."

But Father brought the subject up first. He'd read about it in the local newspaper, and thought we should go. Then Dilly asked about the pet show again, and Mother and Father whispered together for a moment.

"Well, Dilly," said Father at last,

"we've decided you *can* enter Swampy for the pet show . . ."

"Yippee!" shouted Dilly.

". . . but *only* if you behave for the rest of this week, and promise not to be naughty on the day – even if Swampy doesn't win. He'll have a lot of competition."

"OK, Father," said Dilly. "I promise."

"You know, Dilly," sighed Father, "if I had a penny for every time you've promised to be good, I'd be the richest dinosaur in the world. Now, what did it say in the paper . . ."

Father read out the details. Anyone who wanted to enter the pet show was supposed to telephone the dinosaur in charge. It gave his number, and his name, which was Mr Dryden.

"Why is that, Father?" asked Dilly.

"It's probably so there won't be too many entrants," said Father. He turned to Mother. "Could you do it, dear? I'm going to be out of the office all day tomorrow."

"I beg your pardon?" Mother had been looking at some letters to do with her work. "Oh, yes, I've got a busy day tomorrow, but I should be able to ring," she said, and went back to reading her letters again.

Later, at bedtime, I heard Father explaining to Dilly about pet shows. He said Dilly would have to make sure both Swampy and his cage were clean, for a start.

"And sometimes the judges want to see how obedient a pet is," he said. "It's not easy winning a prize, Dilly. Swampy's never had any training, so you'll have to work at it."

"I will, Father," said Dilly.

I smiled. I didn't think he would. But I was wrong.

Dilly wasn't the last one to leave school the next day. He rushed out, dragged us home as quickly as he could, then shot upstairs to his room.

A few minutes later he was in the garden with Swampy. Dilly had him on his leash, and walked him up and down, up and down, up and down . . .

"Sit!" he said. "Heel, Swampy!"

It wasn't having much effect, though. Swampy just didn't seem to understand. For a while I thought

Dilly was going to lose his temper . . . but he managed to control himself.

He didn't get angry the next day, either, even though he still couldn't make Swampy do what he wanted. In fact, he really did keep his promise to behave. He wasn't naughty for *three whole days*. I thought it must nearly have *killed* him.

"There, Dilly," said Father. "See what you can do if you only try? I wish every week could be like this."

"I certainly don't," said Mother. She seemed a little cross. "You might not have noticed, but I've been really busy."

It was true. She'd got home late from work a couple of times, and there had been lots to do around the house, as well. Father apologised, and said he would do the ironing.

Soon the big day arrived. Dilly was so excited he could barely keep still. Father helped him clean the cage and get Swampy ready, and then it was time to go.

We got to Dinosaur Park just in time for the parade. There were floats and a band, and it was the sort of thing Dilly usually loves. But today he wasn't

interested. He took no notice of the rides or the stalls, either.

He only had one thing on his mind – the pet show.

"It's over there, I think," said Father.

We walked across to a large tent. Lots of other dinosaurs were heading in the same direction, each of them with a pet or two. Dilly saw his friend Dixie. She was being pulled along by Titan, her sabre-tooth tiger.

An elderly dinosaur was standing by the entrance. He was wearing glasses and holding a clipboard and pen. He

seemed to be checking everyone as they went in. Dilly went up to him, carrying Swampy in his cage.

"And what is your pet's name?" said the dinosaur.

"Swampy," said Dilly with a big smile.

"Umm . . ." said the dinosaur, looking at his clipboard. "I'm afraid there's no Swampy on my list . . ."

"Oh no!" said Mother, suddenly, putting her paw up to her mouth. "I forgot!" Her face had gone bright green.

The dinosaur was Mr Dryden. Mother should have telephoned him to get Swampy entered, but she had been so busy it had slipped her mind. Now Mr Dryden was saying Swampy couldn't be in the pet show.

Mother and Father argued with

him. They told him how hard Dilly had worked, and how good he'd been, but it was no use. His mind was made up.

I kept my eye on Dilly while the grown-ups were talking. First he looked confused. Then he looked worried. And when he saw Mr Dryden shaking his head, he started to look angry.

I put my paws over my ears. I knew what was coming next.

Dilly opened his mouth and . . . that's right, you guessed it, he let rip with an ultra-special, 150-mile-per-hour super-scream, the kind that sends everyone diving for cover. Then when he stopped screaming, he burst into tears. Dilly was really upset.

"There, there," said Mr Dryden, whose glasses had nearly come off. "Perhaps we can work something out. I don't suppose one small swamp lizard would make much of a difference . . ."

Dilly smiled, and walked into the tent. He wasn't as happy as Mother, though. She was so relieved she gave Mr Dryden a kiss. Now it was his turn to go bright green.

Inside the tent it was total chaos.

Dilly's scream had terrified the other pets, and most of them were out of control. Big pets were chasing little pets, and they were all making lots of noise.

The only calm one was Swampy. He was used to Dilly, and the scream hadn't bothered him. So he won first prize, even though he wasn't really any more obedient than usual.

"I'm sorry I didn't telephone Mr Dryden, Dilly," said Mother on our way home. "I promise I'll do it next year."

"Maybe I'll tie a knot in your tail to help you remember," said Dilly with a smile.

"I deserved that," laughed Mother.

But Dilly wasn't listening any more. He was too busy looking at the big red rosette on Swampy's cage.

Dilly Goes to Gym Club

"What's wrong, Dorla?" said Father when I came home from school the other day. "You've got a face as long as a diplodocus."

"Nothing," I said. "I'm all right."

I wasn't really. My best friend Deena and I had split up. She was spending all her time with Dawn, a new dinosaur in our class. Now I had no one to sit next to, or play with at break. So I *was* very miserable. I just didn't want to talk about it.

Father asked me a few more questions, but I didn't say much. Then he made me a snack and a drink, and I took them up to my room. I sat on my bed and read while I ate my swamp worm sandwich. It was nice being alone.

But I didn't stay that way for long.

I heard footsteps running up the stairs, BANG, BANG, BANG. Then someone pushed my door open so hard it hit the wall with a . . . CRASH!

It was Dilly.

"Come on, Dorla," he said with a big smile. "I've got everything ready. I can't *wait* to get started. I've been looking forward to this *all day*."

My heart sank. I had forgotten about Dilly's computer game. He'd been given it for his birthday. It was too difficult for him, and he had been pestering me for ages to help him with it. That morning, I'd finally given in and said I would.

"Not tonight, Dilly," I said. "I'm busy."

"No you're not," he said, his bottom lip starting to quiver. "You're just reading a book."

"Yes, I'm busy reading and I've changed my mind," I said. "Now leave me alone, will you?"

"I won't," shouted Dilly. "You *promised*, and I'm not moving from here until you play with me!"

Suddenly I lost my temper. I *hate* it when Dilly gets like that. Besides, it had been a bad day, and the last thing I needed was Dilly giving me a hard time.

"Oh yes you are," I shouted back.

I jumped off my bed and gave him a shove. He tripped over his tail and landed with a BONK! on the floor.

Of course, I should have known what would happen next. Dilly opened his mouth and . . . blasted off an ultra-special, 150-mile-per-hour super-scream, the kind that brings Father running as fast as he can.

"What on *earth* is going on up here?" he said. Dilly had stopped screaming, and was crying now. "It sounds like World War 3 has broken out!"

Dilly pointed at me.

"Dorla . . . pushed . . . me . . . over . . ." he said between sniffs and sobs.

"Well, Dorla?" said Father, giving me a stern look. "Did you?"

I admitted I had.

Father soon found out why we'd been arguing. He told Dilly off for screaming, and said he shouldn't expect others to play with him whenever he wanted. But he was more cross with me.

"You shouldn't make promises if you're going to break them, Dorla," he said. "And you certainly shouldn't have pushed Dilly over. Now say you're sorry."

"I'm sorry, Dilly," I said.

But I didn't really mean it.

I felt even more fed up now. Not only had I lost my best friend, I'd also got into trouble because of my horrible little brother. As a punishment, Father said *I* wasn't allowed to watch my favourite programme that evening.

I often wish I was my parents' *only* little dinosaur.

Things weren't going to get any better, either. At breakfast the next morning, Mother reminded me of something I would rather have forgotten. It was the day of our weekly visit to the Community Centre down at The Swamp.

Usually I love going there. Mother does aerobics, Father plays tail ball, Dilly goes to his gym club, Little Leap-

O-Saurs, and I have dance class. Then we all go swamp wallowing, and to MacDinosaurs afterwards for a bronto-burger.

I didn't want to be in my dance class any more, though. I'd always gone with Deena, but now Dawn had joined. They would probably stick together, and make me feel left out. Mother was very surprised when I told her I wanted to give it up.

"But why, Dorla?" she said. "I thought you loved dancing!"

I *do* love dancing, so it was very hard for me to come up with a good reason. I think that's why Mother and Father got suspicious. They managed to get the truth out of me in the end.

"*Now* I see why you've been so bad-tempered," said Father, putting his arm round my shoulders. "Never mind, Dorla. I'm sure you'll make friends with Deena again soon."

I wasn't so sure, although I hoped he was right. He also said he didn't mind if I missed dance class for a couple of weeks.

"That gives us a bit of a problem, though . . ." said Mother. "We can't leave you at home on your own, Dorla. And I don't think we've got time to find a babysitter."

"I hadn't thought of that," said Father. "We'll have to find something else for you to do."

But Mother and Father couldn't think of anything. While we were talking, Dilly was slurping away at his fern flakes and pineapple juice. Then he looked up and smiled.

"I know," he said. "Dorla can come to Little Leap-O-Saurs with me."

"What a good idea!" said Mother. "Dilly, you're a genius!"

I didn't agree. As far as I was concerned Dilly was a pain. I said I would rather be *dead* than go to Little Leap-O-Saurs. It's for *babies*, not dinosaurs my age.

Then I thought about dance class, and anything would be better than that.

On the way to the Community Centre, I was so fed up I thought I would never be happy again. Dilly was all smiles, though. Father said that me being there to play with him at Little Leap-O-Saurs would make his day.

"This way, Dorla," said Dilly when we arrived.

He grabbed my paw and started dragging me towards the small hall where Little Leap-O-Saurs was held. Mother and Father said they would pick us up later.

"Hello, Dilly!" said a friendly-looking lady dinosaur at the small hall. "And who's this you've brought with you today?"

"It's my big sister, Dorla," said Dilly, proudly. "I'm going to show her all the things I can do."

The lady dinosaur's name was Mrs Dundee, and she asked me if I'd like to be her helper. I said I would.

It turned out to be quite a lot of fun, too. I helped Dilly and his little friends climb on all the apparatus. Then we played Catch-The-Tail and Dinosaur Chase. Dilly won both games, and didn't misbehave once.

He had a great time, and so did I.

Which is why I didn't notice two dinosaurs come into the hall. I was quite surprised when one of them spoke to me.

"Is that your little brother?" she said.

I turned round and found myself looking at . . . Dawn! Deena was just behind her.

"Er . . . yes, it is," I said.

"He's so cute, isn't he?" said Dawn, smiling.

I hate it when people say that. Still, I had to admit that maybe today Dawn was right. We got talking, and Dawn asked me all about my family.

"You're so lucky!" she said after a while. "There's only me . . . I wish *I* had a little brother."

I nearly said she could have mine. But I thought about it, and I didn't. Just then Dilly ran over.

"Come on, Dorla," he said, taking my paw. "We're going to play another game now. Do your friends want to join in, too?"

I looked at Dawn and Deena. They both smiled, and nodded.

"Yes, they do," I said.

Dilly ran off, and the three of us

followed him. Somehow I knew that I'd be going to dance class again next week . . .

At home that evening, I helped Dilly with his computer game. He was really pleased, and I enjoyed it too.

I never thought I'd hear myself saying this . . . but little brothers *do* have their uses sometimes.

Even mine!

Have you read these other books about me?

Tony Bradman

DILLY GOES SWAMP WALLOWING

previously published as
Dilly the Worst Day Ever

In this fifth collection of stories about Dilly, the world's naughtiest dinosaur, Dilly causes mayhem at the library, goes swamp wallowing and promises to be good for a whole year – but I don't think he can be, do you?

Tony Bradman

DILLY GOES ON HOLIDAY

Dilly and his family are off on holiday to the Swamp Land theme park. Dilly is sure he's going to have fun – but isn't too pleased when he finds that he's going to have to join the Tiny Tails. Then Dilly meets Dee who looks after the Tiny Tails – and decides that he's going to have a good holiday after all!

In this tenth book about Dilly the Dinosaur, Dilly also takes part in a Sports Day, puts on a magic show and finds a pet.

MEET THE WORLD'S NAUGHTIEST DINOSAUR

Even though, as everyone knows, he's the world's naughtiest dinosaur, Dilly still has lots of fans. Now that he is so famous he's started making special visits to bookshops to meet the people who enjoy reading about him. You might be able to meet him in your local bookshop – he usually tries to behave himself!

You can write to this address for more information about Dilly and his books and about other books published by MAMMOTH.

MAMMOTH Press Office,
38 Hans Crescent,
London SW1X 0LZ

A Selected List of Fiction from Mammoth

While every effort is made to keep prices low, it is sometimes necessary to increase prices at short notice. Mandarin Paperbacks reserves the right to show new retail prices on covers which may differ from those previously advertised in the text or elsewhere.

The prices shown below were correct at the time of going to press.

☐ 7497 1421 2	**Betsey Biggalow is Here!**	Malorie Blackman	£2.99
☐ 7497 0366 0	**Dilly the Dinosaur**	Tony Bradman	£2.99
☐ 7497 0137 4	**Flat Stanley**	Jeff Brown	£2.99
☐ 7497 0983 9	**The Real Tilly Beany**	Annie Dalton	£2.99
☐ 7497 0592 2	**The Peacock Garden**	Anita Desai	£2.99
☐ 7497 0054 8	**My Naughty Little Sister**	Dorothy Edwards	£2.99
☐ 7497 0723 2	**The Little Prince (colour ed.)**	A. Saint-Exupery	£3.99
☐ 7497 0305 9	**Bill's New Frock**	Anne Fine	£2.99
☐ 7497 1718 1	**My Grandmother's Stories**	Adèle Geras	£2.99
☐ 7497 2395 5	**Flow**	Pippa Goodheart	£2.99
☐ 7497 0041 6	**The Quiet Pirate**	Andrew Matthews	£2.99
☐ 7497 1930 3	**The Jessame Stories**	Julia Jarman	£2.99
☐ 7497 0420 9	**I Don't Want To!**	Bel Mooney	£2.99
☐ 7497 1496 4	**Miss Bianca in the Orient**	Margery Sharp	£2.99
☐ 7497 0048 3	**Friends and Brothers**	Dick King Smith	£2.99
☐ 7497 0795 X	**Owl Who Was Afraid of the Dark**	Jill Tomlinson	£2.99

All these books are available at your bookshop or newsagent, or can be ordered direct from the address below. Just tick the titles you want and fill in the form below.

Cash Sales Department, PO Box 5, Rushden, Northants NN10 6YX.
Fax: 01933 414047 : Phone: 01933 414000.

Please send cheque, payable to 'Reed Book Services Ltd.', or postal order for purchase price quoted and allow the following for postage and packing:

£1.00 for the first book, 50p for the second; **FREE POSTAGE AND PACKING FOR THREE BOOKS OR MORE PER ORDER.**

NAME (Block letters) ....

ADDRESS ....

....

☐ I enclose my remittance for ....

☐ I wish to pay by Access/Visa Card Number ☐☐☐☐☐☐☐☐☐☐☐☐☐☐☐☐

Expiry Date ☐☐☐☐

Signature ....

Please quote our reference: MAND